12/22

YASMIN

FIGURES IT OUT!

written by
SAADIA FARUQI

illustrated by
HATEM ALY

PICTURE WINDOW BOOKS
a capstone imprint

To Mariam for inspiring me,
and Mubashir for helping me find
the right words —S.F.

To my sister, Eman, and her amazing
girls, Jana and Kenzi —H.A.

Published by Picture Window Books, an imprint of Capstone.
1710 Roe Crest Drive
North Mankato, Minnesota 56003
capstonepub.com

Text copyright © 2023 by Saadia Faruqi.
Illustrations copyright © 2023 by Capstone.

Library of Congress Cataloging-in-Publication Data is available on the Library of Congress website.

ISBN: 9781666382457 (paperback)
ISBN: 9781666382464 (eBook PDF)

Summary: Join Yasmin in four new adventures that put her courage and problem-solving skills to the test! At home, Baba's got a mystery ailment, and Nani thinks there's a thief afoot. At the farm, Yasmin is put in charge of the chicks—but one goes missing! And at the ice rink, Yasmin puts on a brave face and tries something new. No matter the challenge, puzzle, or mystery, Yasmin gives her all to figure it out!

Design Elements:
Shutterstock: LiukasArt, design element

Printed and bound in the USA. 4802

TABLE OF CONTENTS

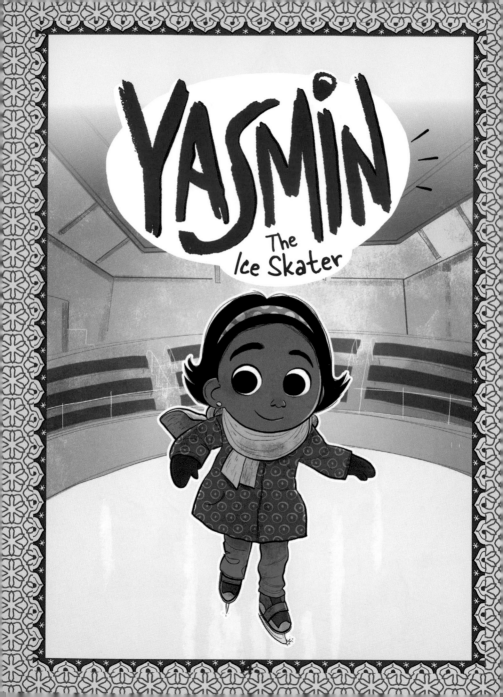

CHAPTER ONE

A New Activity

One Saturday, Yasmin went on a playdate with Emma.

"Guess where we're going?" Emma's mother asked the girls.

Yasmin loved guessing games.

"Go-karting?" Yasmin asked. She liked to go fast!

"Or the trampoline park?" She liked to jump high!

Mrs. Winters laughed. "Good guesses, but this is better," she said. "We're going ice skating!"

Yasmin's stomach filled with bubbles. She'd never skated before. Skating on ice sounded dangerous.

"Great!" Yasmin said, trying to smile.

She didn't want Emma to know
she was scared.

Soon, they came to a big
building. It was cold inside. Lots of
happy families were skating around
the rink. They made it look so easy.

Mrs. Winters bought tickets and rented skates. The skates were heavy, and they had sharp blades on the bottom.

Yasmin gulped. How could she tell Emma she was scared to try skating?

CHAPTER TWO

The Ice Rink

Mrs. Winters helped the girls put on their skates. Then they all held hands as they walked toward the ice.

"Let's go skate!" Emma squealed with excitement.

"Can I get a drink of water first?" Yasmin asked.

"Of course," Mrs. Winters said.

She passed Yasmin a water bottle

from her bag.

Yasmin drank as slowly as she

could.

Then they headed toward the rink once more. They passed a concession stand. "How about some snacks?" Yasmin asked.

"We'll get popcorn later," Mrs. Winters said.

At the edge of the rink, Mrs. Winters stopped to talk to a friend.

Emma stepped onto the ice and started skating. "Come on, Yasmin!" she shouted.

Yasmin saw a big screen on the wall. Her favorite cartoon was playing. "I'll be right there!" she shouted back.

While Emma skated loops around the rink, Yasmin watched the cartoon. Too soon, it ended. Finally, Yasmin knew she had to step onto the ice.

Her feet went forward, and the rest of her went backward.

Crash!

Oh no! Now everyone would know she'd never skated before.

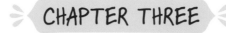

CHAPTER THREE

Learning to Skate

Mrs. Winters came rushing over.

"I don't know how to skate!" Yasmin said miserably.

"It's okay, dear," Mrs. Winters replied, helping her up. "I'll teach you."

She showed Yasmin how to walk safely on the ice. This was called marching.

Then she showed Yasmin how to glide. "Slow and steady," Mrs. Winters said.

When Yasmin fell down, Mrs. Winters showed her how to get up using her hands and knees.

Emma skated over to them. "Want to skate with me, Yasmin?" she asked.

Yasmin wasn't sure she was ready, but she nodded. She didn't want to let Emma down. They held hands tightly and skated slowly around the rink.

"You're doing great, Yasmin!"
Emma said.

They skated together in time
to the music. Everyone looked like
they were having fun. And so was
Yasmin!

The music stopped, and Mrs. Winters waved to them. "Time to go, kids!" she called.

"But I just got started!" Yasmin said as they took off their skates.

Emma laughed. "You spent too much time doing other things, silly."

Mrs. Winters laughed too. "Shall we come back next week?" she asked.

Yasmin nodded. "Yes, please!" she said. Then she pointed to the concession stand. "How about that popcorn now?"

A New Puzzle

One afternoon, Baba brought out a new puzzle.

"Want to join me, Yasmin?" he asked.

Yasmin looked at the box. It had a picture of a village. The box read "1000 Pieces!"

"That's a lot of pieces," Yasmin said.

Baba hugged her. "Don't worry. We'll work on it together."

They set up their work space on the coffee table. "We'll make the edges first," Baba said. "And then we'll fill in the middle."

Yasmin and Baba looked through all 1,000 pieces to find the edges. Every time she spotted a piece with a straight side, Yasmin exclaimed, "Found one!"

As they worked, they sorted the other pieces by color. They kept at it until dinnertime.

Later that evening, Yasmin came to say good night to Baba. He was still working on the puzzle! His back was bent. His eyes were squinted.

"Aren't you tired, Baba?" Yasmin asked, yawning.

Baba didn't even look up. "Just a few more pieces, jaan," he murmured. "Night, night."

Not Feeling Well

The next morning, Baba was lying in bed. Yasmin came to find out why he wasn't at breakfast.

"I feel all achy," Baba said.

"Let me fix you, Baba," Yasmin said. She went to get her doctor's bag.

Yasmin took his temperature. She made him open his mouth and say, "Aah." She even checked his pulse.

"How do you know all this, jaan?" Baba asked.

Yasmin smiled. "Ali's dad spoke at our school last week," she explained. "His name is Dr. Tahir. He works at the hospital."

"What did Dr. Tahir say?" Baba asked.

"He always asks his patients lots of questions," Yasmin said. She took a notepad and pen from her kit.

"Tell me your symptoms, please," she said.

Baba groaned. "My back hurts,"
he said. "And my eyes."

Yasmin wrote that down.

"Runny nose or cough?" she
asked.

Baba shook his head no.

"Did you fall down?" she guessed. "Maybe that's why your back hurts."

Baba shook his head again.

"Too much screen time?" Yasmin asked. "That might hurt your eyes."

Just then, Mama came in with some hot chai.

"Let your baba rest, Yasmin," she said.

Doctor's Orders

Yasmin read over her notes in the living room.

She had followed all the advice from Dr. Tahir. But she still didn't know what was wrong with Baba.

Being a doctor was hard.

Yasmin thought she might cheer up Baba by getting more work done on their puzzle. She leaned over and began looking for pieces.

Yasmin hunched her shoulders as she leaned. She squinted her eyes as she tried to find the right pieces. She worked for a long time.

When she finally stood up, her
back twinged. "OW!" she said. Then
she said, "Aha!"

Yasmin ran to her parents' room.

"Baba! Your back is hurting because you worked on the puzzle for too long!" Yasmin said. "And your eyes too!"

Baba laughed and rubbed his back. "I think you're right, jaan! So, how can I get better?" he asked.

"Rest," Yasmin replied. "And no more than an hour a day on puzzles."

Baba gave Yasmin a hug. "That's good advice, Dr. Yasmin!"

CHAPTER ONE

A Visit to the Farm

Yasmin was excited. Today she was visiting a farm for the first time!

"I can't wait to see all the animals," Yasmin said to Mama and Baba. "Especially the baby chicks!"

"You're going to learn a lot today, Yasmin," Baba said. "Listen carefully and follow directions."

"I will," Yasmin promised. She was going to be the best farmer ever!

The farm was huge. There was one red barn, two green tractors, and three big haystacks. And best of all, lots of animals!

Mama pointed to a sign with strawberries and apples on it. "We'll pick some fruit later," she said.

"But where are the baby chicks?" Yasmin asked.

A worker wearing a sun hat walked up to them. "The baby chicks are in their pen," he said, smiling. "I'm Farmer Tomás. Would you folks like to help with some chores?"

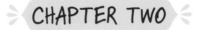

CHAPTER TWO

Helping Out

First, Farmer Tomás took Yasmin and her family to the stables. Yasmin rode a brown horse named Buttercup.

After her ride, Farmer Tomás showed Yasmin how to brush Buttercup's coat until it was smooth and glossy.

Then, they went to see the sheep.

Farmer Tomás showed Yasmin how to

fill their troughs with feed. The sheep

nudged Yasmin's legs. It tickled!

Finally, they reached the chicken coop. There were lots of mama hens and one baba rooster. Near the coop was a pen.

"Look, baby chicks!" Yasmin squealed. "Can I play with them?"

"Of course," Farmer Tomás said. "While you do that, we'll collect the eggs. Please keep the door to the pen closed."

Yasmin nodded. She went into the pen as the others headed to gather eggs. The chicks were even cuter up close!

Yasmin counted the chicks. One, two . . . seven baby chicks!

They pecked at the straw, looking for worms. They climbed over one another. One climbed onto the water dish! Yasmin giggled.

"Be good, chicks!" she said.

Cheep cheep! they replied.

Yasmin sat carefully on the ground. Looking after baby chicks was hard work.

She counted them again. One, two . . .

Uh-oh! Now there were only six chicks in the pen. Where was the seventh one?

CHAPTER THREE

Chick in Trouble

Yasmin searched everywhere. She looked under the straw. She looked in the water dish. She looked behind big bags of seeds. No baby chick!

Then Yasmin saw that the door to the pen was open.

What would Farmer Tomás say? He'd trusted Yasmin to take care of the chicks. What would the mama hens and baba rooster think? She'd lost one of their babies!

Yasmin took a deep breath.
Farmers didn't cry. She searched
outside the pen. She looked under
a wheelbarrow. She peeked inside a
pail.

Then she heard a tiny sound.

Cheep cheep!

The missing chick! There it was,
hiding under a bush. Yasmin picked
it up and held it close.

Farmer Tomás came over with Mama and Baba. "What happened?" he asked.

"I'm sorry I forgot to close the door," Yasmin whispered.

Farmer Tomás smiled. "We all make mistakes, Yasmin," he said. "The important thing is that you found the chick, like a good farmer."

Baba hugged Yasmin. "I'm proud of you, jaan."

"You must be hungry, Farmer Yasmin," Mama said. "Let's go pick some strawberries."

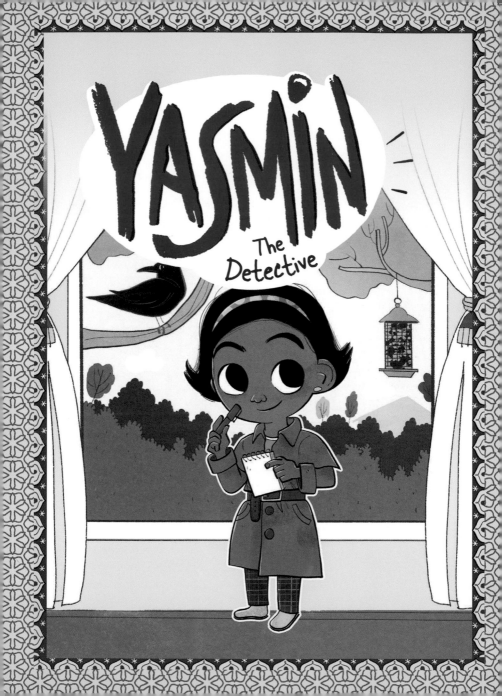

Something Missing

It was a beautiful Saturday. The sun was shining. The birds were chirping.

Nani was sewing, and Nana was reading.

Yasmin was helping Baba put up a new bird feeder.

"Done!" said Baba.

Nana looked up. "Birds are very clever," he said. "They can make and use tools."

"And they can recognize people!" Yasmin said. "We're learning about birds in school."

Yasmin realized it was time for her favorite cartoon. It was about an owl named Detective Hoo. He solved mysteries.

Yasmin headed inside. Soon Nani came in too. She looked confused.

"Have you seen my thimble?" she asked.

"I'll help you look," Yasmin said. Detective Hoo was always searching for missing things.

"Where did you last see it?" Yasmin asked.

"It was on the table outside, and then it was gone," Nani replied.

Yasmin went outside. She looked everywhere. On the table. On the chairs. Even in the grass. No thimble. Where could it have gone?

Detective Work

The next day, birds were fluttering around the new feeder. Some were white. Others were gray. One had a red belly. Yasmin drew them all in her journal.

A big black crow sat on the grass watching her. "Caw, caw!" Yasmin called to it.

After lunch, Nani was puzzled again. "One of the big buttons from my sewing box is missing," she grumbled. "And I can't find my glasses!"

Yasmin had an idea. She got out her journal, just like Detective Hoo.

"Don't worry Nani," she said. "Detective Yasmin is on the case!"

Yasmin interviewed everyone. "Have you seen Nani's missing things?" she asked.

Mama shook her head. "I haven't left the kitchen all morning."

Baba was in the garage. "I'm
sorry, jaan," he said. "I just got back
from the grocery store."

"I've been reading all day," Nana
said, holding up his book.

This was a real mystery. Where could Nani's missing things be? Yasmin would have to hunt for more clues.

CHAPTER THREE

A Break in the Case

On Monday, Ms. Alex showed the class pictures of birds.

"Some birds collect things," she explained.

Emma raised her hand. "What sorts of things?" she asked.

"Food. Or soft things like lint to make their nests cozy," Ms. Alex replied. "Some birds collect shiny objects."

Yasmin's eyes grew big. Nani's thimble, button, and glasses were all shiny. Yasmin had her first clue!

After school, Yasmin took her journal and binoculars to the backyard. Nani and Baba were sitting on the patio.

"Hello, Yasmin," Baba said.

"Shh," Yasmin said. "I'm doing detective work." She hid behind a bush and watched the birds around the feeder.

Caw! said a crow. Was it the same one from yesterday?

"You're my suspect!" Yasmin said as she popped out from behind the bush.

The crow flew to a tree. Yasmin used her binoculars. She saw its nest high in the branches.

"Baba!" she said. "I need a ladder, please!"

"A ladder? Why, jaan?" Baba asked.

"I'm about to solve a mystery!" Yasmin said.

Soon, Baba came back down. He was holding three shiny objects: a thimble, a button, and a pair of glasses.

"Nani's things!" Yasmin cried. "That crow was the thief!"

Nani hugged her. "Shukriya!" she said. "You solved the mystery, Detective Yasmin!"

Think About It, Talk About It

✳ Imagine you are teaching a newbie how to do your favorite activity. What are some tips you would give them?

✳ Have you ever worked on a puzzle with 1,000 pieces? What are some techniques you would use to finish it?

✳ Farmer Tomás tells Yasmin, "We all make mistakes." Think about a time you made a mistake. What did you do to fix it?

✳ Yasmin's knowledge about birds helps her solve the case of Nani's missing items. What facts does she learn that make her think the crow might be the suspect?

Learn Urdu with Yasmin!

Yasmin's family speaks both English and Urdu. Urdu is a language from Pakistan. Maybe you already know some Urdu words!

baba (BAH-bah)—father

chai (CHYE)—tea with milk and spices

hijab (HEE-jahb)—scarf covering the hair

jaan (JAHN)—life; a sweet nickname for a loved one

kameez (kuh-MEEZ)—long tunic or shirt

kitaab (kee-TAHB)—book

lassi (LAH-see)—a yogurt drink

nana (NAH-nah)—grandfather on mother's side

nani (NAH-nee)—grandmother on mother's side

salaam (sah-LAHM)—hello

shukriya (shuh-KREE-yuh)—thank you

Pakistan Fun Facts

Yasmin and her family are proud of their Pakistani culture. Yasmin loves to share facts about Pakistan!

Islamabad

PAKISTAN

Pakistan is on the continent of Asia, with India on one side and Afghanistan on the other.

Many languages are spoken in Pakistan, including Urdu, English, Saraiki, Punjabi, Pashto, Sindhi, and Balochi.

Pakistan has nearly 230,000,000 people. It has the fifth largest population in the world.

Malala Yousafzai and Abdus Salam are two people who won the Nobel Prize from Pakistan.

Mallak Zafar is the first figure skating champion from Pakistan. She began training when she was just five years old!

Make Ice Paint!

SUPPLIES:

- tap water
- ice cube tray
- various colors of food coloring
- craft sticks
- paper to paint on
- newspaper

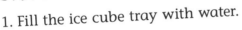

STEPS:

1. Fill the ice cube tray with water.

2. Add a drop of red food coloring to one section and stir with a craft stick. Do this in each section, using a new color and stick each time.

3. You can also mix and match drops of food coloring in the other sections to make new colors. A drop of red and a drop of blue together will make purple. Yellow and red will make orange.

4. Place a craft stick into the middle of each ice cube mold.

5. Freeze at least 4–6 hours.

6. Lay down newspaper under the painting paper.

7. Pull on the craft sticks to remove them from the ice cube tray and use them to paint a picture!

About the Author

Saadia Faruqi is a Pakistani American writer, interfaith activist, and cultural sensitivity trainer featured in *O, The Oprah Magazine*. She also writes middle grade novels, such as *Yusuf Azeem Is Not A Hero*, and other books for children. Saadia is editor-in-chief of *Blue Minaret*, an online  magazine of poetry, short stories, and art. Besides writing books, she also loves reading, binge-watching her favorite shows, and taking naps. She lives in Houston, Texas, with her family.

About the Illustrator

Hatem Aly is an Egyptian-born illustrator whose work has been featured in multiple publications worldwide. He currently lives in beautiful New Brunswick, Canada, with his wife, son, and more pets than people. When he is not dipping cookies in a cup of tea or staring at blank pieces of paper, he  is usually drawing books. One of the books he illustrated is *The Inquisitor's Tale* by Adam Gidwitz, which won a Newbery Honor and other awards, despite Hatem's drawings of a farting dragon, a two-headed cat, and stinky cheese.